CHARLIE ANDERSON

Chris-

Thank you for a great week!

God bless you.
Elaine
August '93
Literacy Conference

CHARLIE ANDERSON

Barbara Abercrombie
illustrated by Mark Graham

Margaret K. McElderry Books
NEW YORK

Margaret K. McElderry Books
Macmillan Publishing Company
866 Third Avenue
New York, NY 10022

Printed in Hong Kong by South China Printing Company (1988) Ltd.

10 9 8 7 6 5 4 3 2

Library of Congress Cataloging-in-Publication Data

Abercrombie, Barbara.
Charlie Anderson.
Summary: A cat comes out of the night to steal the hearts of two sisters who look forward to his sleeping on their beds, until one day Charlie doesn't come home and they learn a surprising secret about him.
[1. Cats—Fiction] I. Graham, Mark, ill.
II. Title.
PZ7.A1614Ch 1990 [E] 89-2449
ISBN 0-689-50486-1

For J.D. and Max
B. A.

To Lauren and Whitney and Jesse
M. G.

One cold night a cat walked out of the woods, up the steps, across the deck, and into the house where Elizabeth and Sarah lived.

He curled up next to their fireplace to get warm.

He watched the six o'clock news on TV.

He tasted their dinner.

He tried out their beds.

He decided to stay, and the girls named him Charlie.
Every morning Charlie disappeared into the woods again.

At night when he came home, Elizabeth brushed him clean, fed him dinner, and made a space for him at the foot of her bed.

He liked Elizabeth's bed the best. Sometimes she would wake up in the middle of the night and hear him purring in the dark.

Sarah called him Baby

and dressed him up in doll clothes.

When it snowed, Elizabeth and Sarah's mother heated Charlie's milk before he left for the woods.

He grew fatter and fatter, and every day he purred louder and louder.

On weekends the girls stayed with their father and stepmother in the city. They wanted to bring Charlie with them, but their mother said he'd miss the woods. "Charlie's a country cat," she told them.

One stormy night Charlie didn't come home. Elizabeth and Sarah stayed out on the deck and called and called his name. But no Charlie.

Where was he? Why wouldn't he come out of the woods? Was he all right?

All night long Elizabeth listened to the rain beating on the roof and the wind rattling the windows. Was he cold? Was he hurt? Where was Charlie?

In the morning Elizabeth and Sarah looked for him. They asked the lady down the road if she'd seen their cat. She said no, and offered them cookies. But they were too worried to eat anything, even her chocolate-chip cookies.

They went to the new house on the other side of the woods. "Have you seen our cat?" they asked. "His name is Charlie. He's very fat and has gray striped fur."

"We have a cat with gray striped fur," said the man. "But his name's not Charlie, it's Anderson. He's upstairs, asleep on our bed."

They heard a meow, and down the stairs came a very fat cat with gray striped fur.

"Charlie!" Sarah and Elizabeth cried.

"No, that's Anderson," said the woman. "We've had him for seven years. Right, Anderson?"

He looked at her and began to purr.

"But it's *Charlie*," Sarah said.

He looked at her and purred louder.

"Is he ever here at night?" Elizabeth asked.

"Anderson is a hunter," said the man. "He prowls the woods at night."

"Charlie sleeps in my bed at night," Elizabeth said. "He leaves for the woods after breakfast."

"Anderson comes home at breakfast time," said the woman. "He leaves right after dinner." They all looked at the cat. He sat at their feet, very happy and very fat.

They call him Charlie Anderson now.

Sometimes, in bed at night, Elizabeth asks him, "Who do you love best, Charlie Anderson?" And she can hear him purring in the dark.

Just like Elizabeth and Sarah,
Charlie has two houses,
two beds,
two families who love him.
He's a lucky cat.